This book
belongs to

....

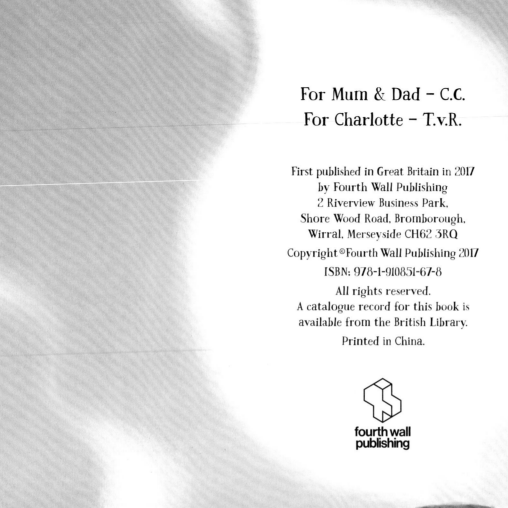

For Mum & Dad – C.C.
For Charlotte – T.v.R.

First published in Great Britain in 2017
by Fourth Wall Publishing
2 Riverview Business Park,
Shore Wood Road, Bromborough,
Wirral, Merseyside CH62 3RQ

Copyright © Fourth Wall Publishing 2017

ISBN: 978-1-910851-67-8

Printed in China.

fourth wall
publishing

Doctor James McGee
and the Time Machine

Written by **Chris Capstick**   Illustrated by **Tom van Rheenen**

Did you ever hear the story
about a rather special little boy
known as 'Doctor' James McGee?

Well, his parents are both very clever scientists
who love to work on top-secret experiments.

It must run in the family,
because James loves science too.
He even has a PHD in:

*Building Inventions out of
sticks, string and glue.*

Well, one bright and early morning
as James was driving into school
(I told you he was special!)
his dad called from his secret lab.

"Oh, we have a huge emergency.
The time machine is frazzled and
it's acting totally crazy!" he yelled.

"Don't worry, Dad." said James,
"We're on our way!"

With speed as quick as lightning,
James activated the car's wings
and powered up the turbo jets
before taking off into the sky
with a mighty WHOOSH!

In no time at all, he landed the car outside the lab and ran inside at full speed.

But as soon as James stepped through the door, he was ZAPPED by the time machine's laser beams!

His parents screamed and ran to help, but before they could get to him, James vanished with an almighty 'POP!'

ARRGHH!

The next second, James was flying down a tube of light, rushing backwards through time...

...before he crash-landed into the tangly vines of an enormous tree.

James had no idea where, or even *when* he was.

That was until he saw some fiery hot volcanoes – and lots of DINOSAURS!

Suddenly, the ground began to shake and rumble. The terrified dinosaurs started to run – heading straight for James!

"Uh-Oh!" said James,
"It's a VOLCANIC ERUPTION!"

James needed a plan, and fast!

He rummaged through his pockets full of calculators, sticks and rubber bands before finally catching hold of some...

"String? That's it!" he shouted.

WHOO-HOO!

With no time to waste, James tied the string into a big lasso and then, as Tyrannosaurus Rex ran by, James captured him!

He leapt onto T-Rex's back
and they raced off through the
growing cloud of flying stones,
molten rock and ash.

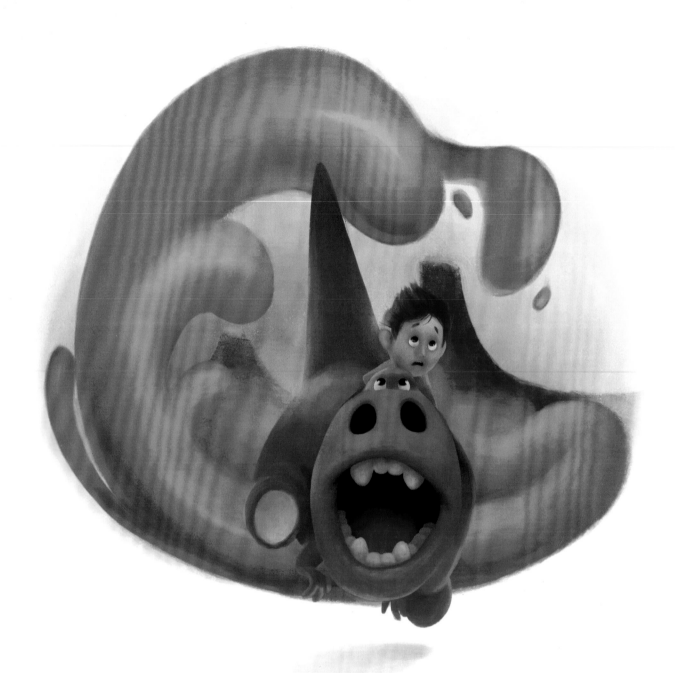

Rex was running as fast as he could,
but the boiling river of red hot lava
was catching them up!

Then James had an idea...

"The sea!" he shouted. He steered the mighty T-Rex towards the rugged coast, and just in time, they JUMPED!...

WEEEE!

...and landed with a big SPLASH!

Below the rolling ocean waves,
everything seemed so peaceful.

That was until the pair were
gobbled up by a giant fishy beast!

The huge old fish swam on for days with James and Rex in his tummy. Finally, he came up to the surface to breathe.

This was just what James and Rex had been waiting for. They dashed out of the monster's mouth and escaped back onto land!

But they had no idea where they were,
and the weather was sub-zero!

When a blizzard began to cover them in ice
and snow, they found it hard to carry on...

...eventually, they were frozen stiff
and turned to blocks of ice.

Now how will poor frozen James escape
his journey back through time!?

Meanwhile, back at their secret lab,
James' parents had been working
non-stop to fix the time machine.

But as the days passed by, they
began to worry they might never
see their little boy again...

...that was until their friend came running
in waving the newspaper headlines...

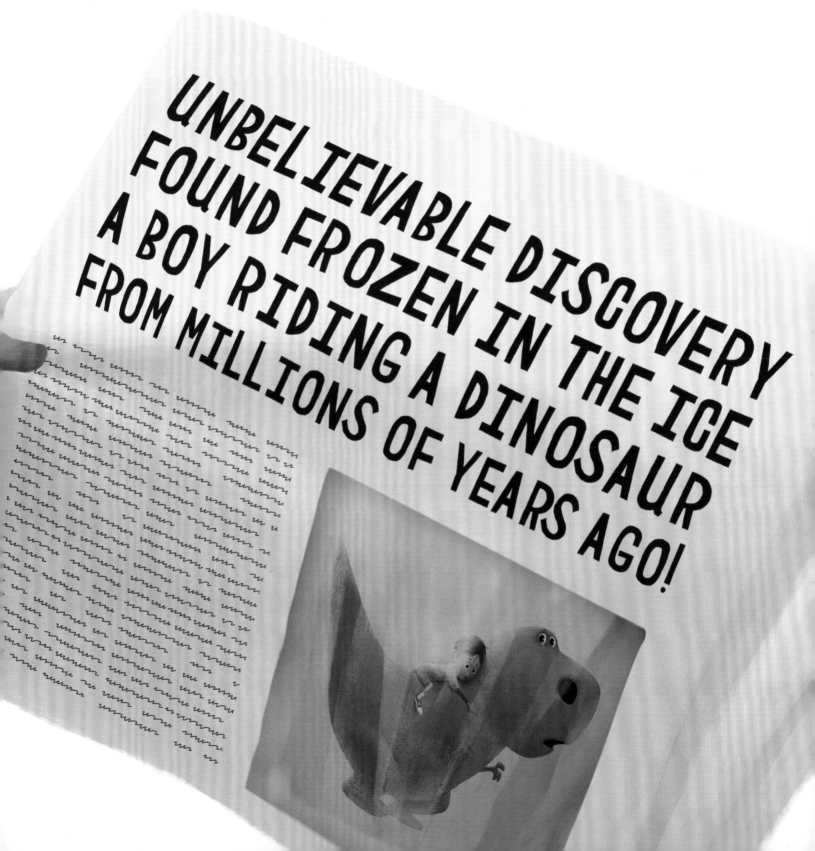

UNBELIEVABLE DISCOVERY
FOUND FROZEN IN THE ICE
A BOY RIDING A DINOSAUR
FROM MILLIONS OF YEARS AGO!

With tears of happiness running down
their cheeks, James' parents jumped
into their flying car.

"The North Pole right away!" they said,
"Let's go get our little boy."

Back at home, the giant ice cube was melted to the floor, and out stepped Doctor James McGee with his new pet dinosaur.